# Captain Peaches
## Storms the
## Delaware Beaches

**MAINSTAY PUBLISHING**

Denise Blum  Lisa Sanderson

Written by Denise Blum.  Illustrated by Valerie Cianfaro.

Printed in the USA.

Mainstay Publishing
P.O. Box 293
Middletown, DE 19709
(302) 223-6636
publisher@mainstaypublishing.com
www.mainstaypublishing.com

ISBN 978-0-9832901-2-4

It was an ordinary day at Pirate Cove School.
Peaches sat quietly upon her wood stool.

The teacher droned on about history and such.
But none of that mattered to Peaches too much.

1

The teacher told stories of times long ago,
of people and places that students should know.
Of old pirate warriors and big famous ships,
of schooners and frigates and brave ocean trips.
Peaches dreamed of the future, she longed to explore.
She dreamed of excitement, adventures galore!

2

Suddenly her teacher said something new.
Peaches perked up, curiosity grew.

"Treasure be buried a long time ago
by the famous ole cap'n, Edward Mako.

His treasure be hidden, it's never been found.
Scallywags and rogues have looked all around.
Avast, it's still out there! See the map in this book?
I'll pass it around. Take a good look."

3

Peaches saw the map and knew right away
that adventure would come the very next day.

She would find Mako's treasure. She'd hunt and explore.
She'd find diamonds and rubies and emeralds and more!

The top of the map read "The Delaware Beaches."
"That's where I'm headed," announced Captain Peaches.

The X was the key to finding the loot.
Peaches studied the map and planned out her route.

Peaches readied her ship and gathered her crew.
They sailed through the ocean as the wind blew.
The gusts grew stronger and the sky turned dark grey.
A big storm rolled in and made the boat sway.
A sea monster leapt in front of the ship.
They almost capsized! What a dangerous trip!

But the crew was determined, they wouldn't turn back.
The thought of treasure kept them on track.

Then one day "Land Ho!" announced Captain Peaches.
They had finally arrived at the Delaware Beaches!

# ARRRGGGHHHHH!

Readers, can you help me?
Put on your thinking cap.

Help me find the big red X
from the treasure map!

7

Peaches looked at the treasure map. "I see our first stop!"
"It's just around the corner... King's Ice Cream Shop."

She burst through the front door seeking jewels and gemstones.
Instead she found Italian ice and yummy ice cream cones.

Was Peaches disappointed? Oh no! Not at all!
She made herself an ice cream cone fourteen inches tall!

The map sent the crew to Child's Play by the Bay,
where children learned letters like C, Y and J.

There were kids being taught to read and to write,
learning X is for x-ray and K is for kite.

Peaches said, "X stands
for treasure in the pirate alphabet.
It's the spot on the map that
I haven't found yet!"

9

Peaches stormed into Kids' Ketch and searched the toy jets,
the books and the games and the dainty tea sets.

"Mates, look o'er there! What could that be?"
She said, "Looks like a treasure chest to me!"

Peaches lifted the chest high in the air.
"The booty 'tis ours! Rapscallions beware!"

When she opened the chest she realized her blunder.
It was a toy, there was no pirate plunder.

The Cape May - Lewes Ferry was the next place they explored.
The pirates ran out to the dock and quickly climbed on board.

They checked the arcade, the lounge, the life boats and sun decks.
From bow to stern they searched the boat. They didn't find an X.

11

At Jake's Seafood, Captain Peaches rooted through crab cakes,
checked all through the salmon and poked around the steaks.

She ran into the kitchen and saw a great big pot.
She moved the lid to peek inside…what a mess she got!

The pot was filled with lobsters. They jumped onto the floor,
scurried 'round the kitchen and headed out the door!

The chef was mad and chased her out with a wooden spoon!
She had no time to hunt for a diamond or doubloon!

The pirates went to the beach and surveyed the ocean,
looked under towels and in suntan lotion.

"I see an X!" Captain Peaches shouted with glee.
"An X made of shovels, come dig with me!"

She burrowed and scraped. She scooped and she dug.
But all she found was a shell and a little beach bug.

"I bet Mako hid his treasure
at Rehoboth Toy & Kite!"
Peaches thought excitedly,
"I really hope I'm right!"

She checked the bubble blowers,
inspected all the flags,
analyzed the wind chimes and
peeked inside beach bags.

No gems, no gold, no booty.
She didn't find a jewel.
But she bought a brand new kite.
That was really cool!

14

At Nicola Pizza they examined the french fries,
cut open Nic-o-bolis and searched through pizza pies.

"No treasure here," she said, "but all the food smells great."
Peaches sat right down and ordered a big plate.

The treasure hunt continued at Lilypad Boutique,
a store filled with kids' clothes, so cute and unique.

They peeked under toys and next to the shirts,
inside the shoe boxes, behind the skirts.

"No treasure here.  Peaches, what should we do?"
"Peaches???  Where's Peaches?" asked one of the crew.

"Over here," shouted Peaches.  She struck a fun pose.
"I'm tired of my outfit.  I bought some new clothes!"

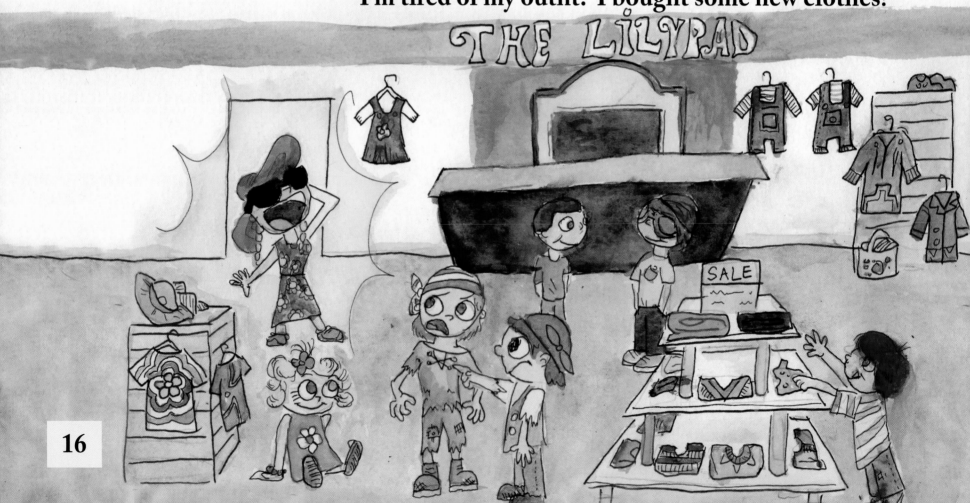

The Boardwalk Plaza Hotel was where they went next.
They searched high and low for the mysterious X.

They looked by the pool and under a chair.
They surveyed the lobby, they looked everywhere!

The restaurant, the beachfront, they looked all around.
But ole' Mako's treasure just couldn't be found!

"Let's try something new," she said. "Let's head out to the street and ask for treasure hunting help from people that we meet."

She saw a man walking out of Bluecoast Seafood Grill. Peaches asked, "Was there an X on your dinner bill?"

A lady strolled toward Matt's Fish Camp.
Peaches grabbed her hand.

"Call me if you find the X.
Check the hostess stand."

She talked to everyone in sight, everyone nearby.
But no one had seen the X. "It was worth a try!"

19

At Fifer Orchards, Peaches felt
like she was in a dream.
"Mates, look at the sign out front.
They sell PEACH ICE CREAM!"

She forgot about the treasure
and ordered a big cone.
Then she visited the orchard
where fresh peaches are grown.

Captain Peaches smiled
as she looked up at a tree.
"This fruit tastes great and,
best of all, it's named after me!"

The crew was getting tired
but Peaches said, "Don't quit!"
"I just checked the treasure map.
Our next stop is Go Brit!"

They headed to Go Fish
and continued on their quest.
Peaches said, "Look everywhere!
Let's find that treasure chest!"

They DID find something special.
Not a jewel or a crown.
It was sticky toffee pudding,
the best dessert in town!

21

Peaches wouldn't give up! She spotted a guy
with a metal detector meandering by.

"Aye Mates, gold is metal. Argh, silver is too!"
"We need that detector," she yelled to the crew.

She grabbed the detector. But to her dismay
the man snatched it back and then stormed away!

22

"Onto Fins Fish House!" Peaches yelled to her crew.
"We must find the fortune before scallywags do!"

They burst through the door and spotted a dish
filled with oysters and tuna and clams and swordfish.

"We studied oysters in school. They grow pearls inside!
Pearls are gems. Gems are treasure. Grab them!" she cried.

The crew checked the oysters but all that they found
was somebody's dinner. No pearls were around.

23

The pirates entered Dos Locos ready for lunch.
Stonegrill steak and fajitas… they ordered a bunch!

Quesadillas and tacos filled with fresh fish.
A frisbee to eat from instead of a dish!

Frisbees for plates?!? Peaches thought that was neat.
"Let's play!" she said as she jumped to her feet.

24

They sailed to the Indian River Inlet Bridge
but they didn't find treasure, not even a smidge.

Tidepool Toys was on the map, near the oceanfront.
Peaches thought, "The perfect place for a treasure hunt!"

The pirates combed through games and balls. They looked at cars and bats.
They fumbled through the hoola hoops, the costumes and the hats.

"Readers, do you know where Mako hid his treasure chest?
Did you find the big red X? Do you have a guess?"

"We searched Lewes and Rehoboth.
We checked Dewey too.
Bethany and Fenwick were
inspected by my crew."

"Readers, can you help us?
We missed a clue somewhere.
Where is Mako's treasure?
We've looked everywhere!"

The treasure is at...

# ... JAKES SEAFOOD!!!

Peaches said, "We missed the X when we were here before!"
"That's because the angry chef chased us out the door!"

"But now we're back. We found the X. I'm glad the chef's not here!"
She opened up the treasure chest. The crew began to cheer!

The chest was overflowing. It was filled with coins and rings,
jewels and gemstones, bars of gold and lots of sparkly things!

The pirates celebrated. They were happy as can be.
"Yo ho ho! We found our fortune!" Peaches said with glee.

"Mates, it's time to have some fun. Kick off your pirate boots.
Grab towels, beach umbrellas and your bathing suits!"

They went swimming in the ocean, fishing in the bay,
played games on the boardwalk. They had fun all day!

Peaches sipped some pirate grog while lounging in a chair.
She said, "I love the beaches in southern Delaware!"

29

To CB, CB & CB-
XO, XO, & XO -D.B.

Ty, Molly & Sean –
Love you so much!
Is it time for surf
fishing yet? - L.S.

To my friends, family,
and professors that
helped me get this far-
Thank you! -V.C.

## Other Books by Mainstay Publishing...

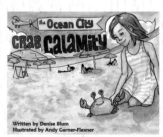

**Check www.mainstaypublishing.com for links to all featured destinations.**